MY
VAMPIRE
GRANDAD

To Kai
Happy reading!
Roxx

THE FANG GANG

MY

VAMPIRE GRANDAD

Roy Apps

Illustrated by

Sumiko Shimakata

BLOOMSBURY

LONDON   NEW DELHI   NEW YORK   SYDNEY

Bloomsbury Publishing, London, New Delhi, New York and Sydney

Published in Great Britain in October 2006 by Bloomsbury Publishing Plc,
50 Bedford Square, London, WC1B 3DP

A CIP catalogue record for this book is available from the British Library

ISBN 978 0 7475 8358 5

Printed in Great Britain by Clays Ltd, St Ives Plc, Bungay, Suffolk

5 7 9 10 8 6

MIX
Paper from
responsible sources
FSC® C018072

www.bloomsbury.com

Chapter 1

THE MORNING MY LIFE changed for ever started off dead normal really.

We were all having breakfast; Dad, Mum and me. Dad was slurping coffee and reading the paper. Mum was nibbling a slice of rye bread and going through her post. I was munching my way through a bowl of Choco Crunchies.

Suddenly, Mum leapt off her chair and

started screaming, 'Ye-es! I've won! I've won! I've WON!!!'

Like I said, it was a dead normal morning.

Dad groaned and carried on reading the paper. I sighed and carried on reading the Choco Crunchies packet. I discovered that each Choco Crunchy contains five point eight calories of energy. Amazing!

'Don't you want to know what it is I've won?' Mum enquired.

'No!' Dad and I shouted, together.

Entering competitions is what my mum does for a living. Every week she wins something. The week before, she had won a singing toilet-roll holder.

When you've done what you must do
Don't forget to flush the loo!

Was what it sung.

So you can see why Dad groaned and I sighed at the thought of another competition win.

'Not even the teeniest, weeniest bit?' Mum asked.

'No, no, NO!' Dad and I shouted, again.

I looked up and saw there was a kind of strange, powerful smile playing about my mum's face.

'Not even if I tell you that it's a three-month luxury cruise to the Antarctic?' she shrieked.

I almost choked on my Choco Crunchies.

'A cruise! Brilliant, Mum! Yeh! Three months off school!' I yelled.

I even thought of going over the top a bit and giving her a hug, but Dad got there first.

Mum put the letter on the table for us to read. This is what it said:

Muck-In-A-Minute Instant Meals

Dear Mrs Leech

We are delighted to inform you that you have won first prize in our recent Name-That-Noodle competition!

Your prize is a romantic holiday of a lifetime for you and your partner – a three-month cruise to the Antarctic!

Yours sincerely

(Ms) R. Snick
Customer Services Manager

Dad started jumping round the kitchen, punching the air with his fists and going: 'Yee–hah! Yee–hah!'

Then he rushed over to Mum and flung his arms round her neck – again – and called her 'darling'.

In order to avoid having to watch this all-time yuckiest moment, I looked down at the table and found myself reading the letter again.

I got to the second paragraph – and stopped. I read it again – and again – and suddenly I came over all sweaty.

Chapter 2

'**M**UM?'

But she was still busy having an all-time yuckiest moment with Dad.

'Excuse me!' I said, loudly.

'Yes, dear?' mumbled Mum, from behind Dad's left ear.

'This romantic cruise you've won. It's only for *two* people.'

'Well, you can hardly have a romantic cruise

for three now, can you?' replied Dad, giving Mum a wink and a soppy smile.

'But what about *me*?'

Mum unhooked herself from Dad and looked up at me with a frown, as if she'd forgotten for the moment just *who* I was, exactly. Dad turned, stared out of the window and started scratching his nose.

'Ahhh,' he said.

'Hmmm,' said Mum, still frowning.

'Perhaps he could be a stowaway?' suggested Dad, brightly.

'What, with *his* chest?' snorted Mum. 'I don't know much about Geography, but I'm sure I read somewhere that the Antarctic can get quite chilly at times. He'd be forever catching cold.'

They're always doing that. Talking about me as if I wasn't there.

'In that case, then,' said Dad, firmly, 'he'll just have to go and stay with your mother.'

'Three months with Gran?' I gasped. 'Couldn't you put me in a field with a raging bull, instead?'

'Don't be silly, dear –'

'It's just that I think I'd prefer to be *gored* to death by a bull, than *bored* to death by Gran,' I replied, quite wittily, I thought. 'I do not want to go and stay with her!'

'The thing is, Jonathan,' began Dad, 'you see, there's no one else you can stay with, is there, apart from your gran.'

Suddenly, Mum's eyes widened and she smiled. I half expected a huge neon sign flashing the word 'IDEA!!!' to appear above her head.

'He could go and stay with your father down in Goolish!' she exclaimed.

'What!' said Dad. And he went a deathly pale. Knowing what I know now, I'm not the least surprised, but at the time I thought it seemed most odd.

'I don't see why not,' Mum continued.

They were doing it again. Talking about me as if I wasn't there.

'You'd send me away to stay with an old man I've never even met?' I yelled.

'Actually, you have met him,' retorted Mum.

'When?' I asked.

'Years ago, when you were a baby. He popped in here to use the loo, on his way to an old people's holiday place in . . . where was it, Kevin?'

'Transylvania,' muttered Dad, with a shiver, adding quickly, 'no, I will not – repeat not – allow Jonathan to go and stay with that v . . . v . . . very old . . . father of mine.'

'OK. If that's how you feel about it.' Mum pouted and shrugged. Her and Dad's all-time yuckiest moment was definitely over. She whipped out her mobile phone, slapped it to her ear and exclaimed, 'Mum? It's Tracey! How would you like to have Jonathan stay with you for a few weeks?'

Just to make my views on the subject perfectly clear, I stormed out of the kitchen, slammed the door and stomped upstairs to my bedroom.

Chapter 3

A ND SO WOULD YOU have, in my place.

It wasn't that I minded being away from home for three months – there was an obvious plus to this – I wouldn't have to go to school! Cool or what?

On the other hand, I would miss my mates, the Princes, Harry and Wills. Prince is their surname; they're not royalty. It's just that when they were born, their mum thought naming them Harry and Wills was too good a chance to miss. She's always coming into school just to see their names in the register, which looks like this:

Patel   Amina
Pratt   Jordanne
Prince   Harry
Prince   Wills

Harry and Wills were both top footballers. And lately, I'd found myself a regular in the school football team. Harry and Wills had discovered that I could make these really fast runs down the full length of the pitch. At the time I put it down to growing up and eating a bowl of Choco Crunchies each morning.

No, the actual nightmare about going to stay with Gran – was *Gran*. So that you can see for yourselves the true horror of the situation, here is a list of her five fave hobbies:

1: Watching gardening programmes on TV
2: Visiting garden centres
3: gardening
4: gardening
5: gardening

See what I mean? *Boring* just doesn't begin to sum it up.

So you can imagine how I felt, when two weeks later, I found myself sitting in Gran's car waiting to be driven off to spend three months in her company.

'Bye, darling! And don't forget to wash your feet!' Mum yelled to me through the passenger window. I slid right down in the seat, just in case anyone from school should be walking along and hear.

Gran revved the engine and slipped the car into gear. Unfortunately, it was reverse gear and we almost ran over Dad, who shouted something I would've been fined four weeks' pocket money for saying.

That's another thing about Gran. Her driving.

13

That's why I didn't talk to her during the journey. I thought it best to let her concentrate on the road ahead. Not to mention the red light ahead. And the articulated lorry pulling out of a side road ahead . . .

For the rest of the journey, I sat with my eyes shut tight.

After we'd arrived and I had taken my stuff upstairs, she said, 'Now I simply must do a supermarket run this afternoon, dear. You can either come with me or stay here.'

I wasn't going to get into Gran's car any more than strictly necessary. Given the standard of her driving, I reckoned it would be safer spending the afternoon in a tank full of piranha fish.

'I'll stay here,' I said.

'Good. Don't worry. I'll only be a couple of hours. You can watch television.'

'Have you got cable, yet?' I asked.

Gran laughed. 'Cable? What do I need cable television for when I've got a garden pond with two gnomes called Paul and Barry, a miniature watermill and a green plastic frog?'

I couldn't think of a polite answer to that.

And, pausing only to collect a shopping trolley from the hall cupboard, Gran marched purposefully out through the front door.

I watched half an old American movie that was so slow it could've sent a snail to sleep. Then I switched channels and watched a programme for very small children. It starred an orange dog and a green cat who sang all ten verses of 'The Wheels on the Bus' in very silly voices. Now I knew where the phrase 'dumb animals' came from.

Still, things weren't all bad. I made out a list of plusses and minuses.

LIFE WITH GRAN LIST

Minsuses	Plusses
Gran	No yucky moments (e.g. Mum and Dad)
No cable telly	NO SCHOOL!!!!!!!
Paul and Barry the garden gnomes	NO SCHOOL!!!!!!!
Plastic frog	NO SCHOOL!!!!!!!

And I realised that the plusses made it all worthwhile, really.

When I looked up at the telly again, there was a programme starring two pink warthogs. Then I rubbed my eyes and saw that they weren't pink warthogs, but the presenters of the Six O'clock News.

Gran had been at the supermarket for over four hours!

I added another minus to my list:

Serious risk of dying of starvation.

Chapter 4

I WAS CHECKING MY face in the hall mirror to see whether lack of food was making me pale and hollow-eyed when I heard the front door go and in came Gran.

'Well, that's the last time I'm going to the supermarket,' she said.

'Why? What happened?'

She went through to the sitting room, flopped down on the settee, flung off her shoes, planted her feet on the coffee table and closed her eyes.

'Oh, nothing to get excited about,' she said, with a sigh. 'But there I was, racing down the aisle to get the last case of special offer Spanish wine, when Mrs Rhode-Hogg from down the road barged past me and got there first. I grabbed the wine off her, then she tried to clout me round the ear with a packet of 48 Super Value Fish Fingers. So I rammed my trolley into her legs and for good measure swiped her over the head with a 20 lb oven-ready turkey.'

'Was she badly hurt?' I asked.

'I'm sorry to say she wasn't,' said Gran, 'but the police charged me with 'Actual Bodily Harm' (to Mrs Rhode-Hogg) and 'Grievous Bodily Harm' (to the frozen turkey).'

Over tea, Gran said, 'I have to go to court tomorrow morning. And then, I shall have to go away.'

'Away? Away where?'

'To prison, of course,' said Gran. 'My lawyer says I'll be inside for three months at least.'

'Don't be silly, Gran,' I said, laughing. 'They won't send you to prison. You'll get an ASBO, that's all.'

Gran shook her head. 'I've already got an ASBO. I got it last month when I shoved a shopping trolley into Mrs Mills-Boon's 4x4. So you see, this time it really is prison for me.'

I wasn't quite sure what to say. But I thought it would be polite to say I was very sorry, so I did.

'Well, don't be,' replied Gran. 'I'm quite looking forward to a nice spell inside. At last I shall be able to catch up with my knitting. The question is, what are we going to do with you? I don't suppose the authorities would let you come to prison with me. Have you got any other relatives you could stay with?'

I shrugged. 'Only, my grandad Leech,' I said. 'But I don't know him very well. He lives in a place called Goolish.'

'That's by the sea,' said Gran, excitedly. 'That'll be nice for you, dear. Have you got his phone number?'

I shook my head.

'Never mind, there can't be that many Leeches in Goolish. I'll try directory enquiries.'

Gran went upstairs to telephone. Ten minutes later she was back downstairs with me.

'Well, that's sorted,' she said.

'What did he say?'

'The line wasn't very good, but I thought I heard him say something about *van hire*,' she said, with a shrug. 'But I explained you hadn't got that much luggage.'

'Are *you* going to drive me to Goolish, then?' I asked with a gulp.

'Would that I could, dear,' said Gran. 'But the police have forbidden me to travel outside the town boundary. Don't worry, I'll hire you a taxi.'

I sighed with relief. 'And did you ask him if he had cable?'

'I did and he has,' said Gran, nodding. 'He said it'll be in your room.'

'Cool!'

'He only had one concern.'

'What was that?'

'He said being that as it was a full moon, you *must* arrive at his house before midnight.'

Chapter 5

I SPREAD MYSELF ON the back seat of the taxi and got to wondering about Grandad Leech. Although, of course, I didn't actually remember meeting him when I was a baby, I did know what grandads were like. Lots of my mates at school had grandads and they were always going on about how they took you swimming, watched football, bought you pizza and stuff like that. And you could bet Grandad Leech wouldn't have two gnomes and a plastic green frog in his front garden.

I re-did my list and it looked like this:

LIFE WITH ~~GRAN~~ GRANDAD LIST

Minsuses	Plusses
~~Gran~~	No yucky moments (e.g. Mum and Dad)
~~No cable telly~~	Cable telly (<u>and</u> computer?)
~~Serious risk of dying of starvation~~	Pizza
~~Paul and Barry the garden gnomes~~	Swimming
~~Plastic frog~~	NO SCHOOL!!!!!!!

Yes, life was beginning to look very good indeed.

The taxi raced on and on for hours. We went through villages, towns and countryside. Grandad Leech lived a long way away. *No wonder Dad had never got round to visiting him*, I thought.

Suddenly, the taxi kind of lurched into a dense forest of overhanging trees. We began descending sharply into a dark valley. The trees gave way to a few houses and at last I saw the road sign. I know we were going fast, but I could have sworn it said:

GOOLISH
Welcomes scareful drivers

The taxi pulled up halfway along a narrow, dead-end lane. There were no street lights.

'Journey's end,' said the taxi driver, with a shiver in his voice. 'You can get your own bags out of the boot. This place gives me the creeps.'

I could see what he meant. It was still and dark. The only sound was the wind blowing through the tall, dark trees which surrounded us.

I got my bags out of the boot. Straightaway the taxi revved up. It did a rapid three-point turn, then with a screech of tyres headed back up the cul-de-sac towards the open road, the boot door still swinging wildly in the air.

I could just about make out the name on the rickety garden gate:

DRAC'S COTTAGE

I made my way slowly up the front path towards the dark and gloomy cottage.

A thin sliver of light flickered from an upstairs window, making it just bright enough to pick out the shadowy form of a

large door knocker. I rapped it loudly on the door. It was rusty and it squeaked. Chips of dirty paint fluttered to the ground. *Grandad Leech must be poor*, I thought, *not to be able to afford paint or proper lights*. Maybe he'd spent all his money on a giant plasma TV screen? I sighed. Deep down, I knew this was just wishful thinking. Something in the pit of my stomach told me there must be a more sinister reason.

A croaky voice from behind the front door hissed, 'Who's there and what do you want?'

'It's me, Jonathan.'

The door creaked open to reveal an ancient man. He was tall and thin with wispy white hair and piercing eyes. His craggy face was the colour of pastry. He peered at me through two long, pointed, shiny teeth.

'Hello, Grandad,' I said.

Chapter 6

'WELCOME TO DRAC'S Cottage, boy,' Grandad said, beckoning me inside with a long crooked finger.

Grandad's hall was small and dark, lit only by the pale glow from upstairs. On a small, rickety table was a vase of decaying flowers. Above the table, on the wall, was one of those old-fashioned telephones you see in films. The sort where you have to turn a handle.

No wonder Gran had complained about the line being bad.

'I'll take your bag,' he said, and in one move he had slung one of my bags over his left shoulder and the other one over his right. I remembered reading somewhere about frail old men who have incredible strength, but this was impressive.

'Follow me!' Grandad called.

Grandad took the steep and creaking stairs two at a time, casting pale dancing shadows on the walls. I followed after him, feeling I'd be less scared if I kept with him, rather than being alone in that dark, eerie hallway.

When we reached the landing Grandad stopped. I started to go into the room from which the light was shining.

'No!' he yelled, his wild eyes staring madly at me. 'NOT in there!' He beckoned me up another narrower, even creakier staircase to the attic.

He flicked on the light switch and the room was revealed in a sickly yellow glow. There was a small wooden bed, a chair, a wardrobe and a huge table. A faded red rug covered the wooden floor. I reckoned Gran would have better stuff in her prison cell.

There was no cable telly.

'Gran said you had er . . . cable?' I said.

'Yes, a beauty, isn't it,' said Grandad, thumping the table with a bony fist. 'Hope you like it.'

'No, not table, *cable* . . .' I began.

Grandad was standing by the window. 'There's a fine view of the graveyard from up here,' he was saying, 'especially when it's a full moon, like tonight.' He turned and peered at me, frowning. My top lip had started to quiver. 'Huh,' he said. 'I hope you're not one of those wimpy kids who are forever getting homesick?'

I shook my head. I'd never felt so homesick in my life.

'I mean,' I said, hoping that somehow the sound of my own friendly voice would suddenly make me feel better, 'I hardly ever see my mum and dad, anyway. Mum's always busy with her competitions . . .'

'And your dad?' snapped Grandad.

'He puts in a lot of hours at a wood yard.'

'Works in a wood yard, does he? What does he make?'

'Oh, fences, stakes, that sort of thing,' I said.

Grandad sniggered and leered at me. 'I might have guessed!'

'And at weekends, he's always up his allotment,' I twittered on, nervously.

'What does he grow? Don't tell me, garlic!'

I nodded. 'How did you know?'

Grandad cackled. 'You mean he hasn't told you?'

'Told me what?' I asked, my heart beating like mad.

But before Grandad could reply, the church

clock began to strike, loudly and mournfully, in the distance.

'Goodness, a quarter to midnight already,' he gasped. His face spread into another wide, toothy grin. 'Now, I expect you're tired after your journey, so I'll leave you to unpack and get some sleep.' He turned towards the door. 'I won't be long.'

'Where are you going?' I asked, my stomach beginning to churn like a cement mixer at the thought of being left all alone.

'Oh, you know, out for a bite . . . er, I mean out for a *bit*.'

'But, Grandad, no! You can't leave me on my own . . . !' I blurted out.

But Grandad was already gone. I heard the front door slam and went to the window. In the moonlight I picked out the faint, darting shape of a tiny creature, like a bat, flitting over the front gate.

After that, silence.

And after *that*, the sound of an occasional but insistent howling that seemed to come

from the direction of the graveyard.

With a feeling of dread and foreboding I did what I always do when I'm worried about something: I made a list.

SCARY STUFF ABOUT MY GRANDAD

He goes on holiday to Transylvania

His teeth!

He wanted me here by *midnight*

His son (my dad) makes stakes for a living and grows garlic for a hobby

He lives in *Drac's* Cottage

He's very strong

Everything seemed to point to the same

conclusion. No . . . I must have got it wrong. Perhaps Grandad was just a funny old man in need of a good dentist?

There was only one way to find out the truth. I crept out of my room, down the narrow wooden stairs to the landing. The dim light was still shining behind the half-open door as it had been since my arrival.

I took two steps towards it. Then, the palms of my hands sticky with sweat, I pushed the door open and stepped inside.

I banged my shin on something.

I looked down and found myself peering into a large, shiny, wooden coffin.

Chapter 7

I FELT SICK, desperate to get out of that dreadful room as soon as possible. But I couldn't. I just stood there, staring at the coffin. It was like when you see roadkill, you don't want to look at it, but something dark inside you makes you look.

Even worse, the bright, shiny wood of the coffin seemed to be saying: 'Go on, touch me! Touch me, if you dare.'

The other thing stopping me leave, of course, was the fact that my shin hurt like mad from when I'd knocked it on the side of the coffin.

Eventually, shaking from head to foot, I took a step back, and another. I reached the door and then, still shaking, clattered down the stairs to the front door. One thought only was on my mind: this was a bad place and I had to get away.

Once outside on the front path I realised it

was a stupid idea. Get away? How? Where? There was no way out of Goolish at this time of night. And as to Goolish itself, I knew nobody in the town. But if they were all like Grandad, I'd be better off staying put until the morning.

I looked up into the night sky. There wasn't a star in sight. Just the full moon casting blue-grey shadows on the garden. At least it was light. Perhaps I should just make a run for it. From the direction of the graveyard, once again, came the sound of an occasional but insistent howling. But this time the howling sounded nearer and the longer I listened the nearer it came.

That decided it. I ran straight back inside the cottage and leaned back against the front door, panting like mad. As well as the howling I could now hear laughter and chattering voices. I turned the key in the lock. And not a moment too soon, because the next thing I knew, the door handle was being forced from outside.

My grandad's voice said: 'Why, knock me down with a gravedigger's spade! The boy's locked the door!'

Then another voice, a woman's, said: 'So, what are we going to do now?' Except the 'now' came out more like 'ner-howl'!

There wasn't a moment to lose. I ran through the hall to the kitchen.

I bumped against the table, tripped over the rubbish bin and banged my already bruised shin against a chair, but I didn't care. I had to escape.

Suddenly, the back door flew open and the kitchen was flooded with light. Standing in the doorway was Grandad.

'Ah, glad you're still up, boy. I've brought a few friends round for tea,' said Grandad through a toothy grin.

He stepped into the kitchen, followed by a man with the thickest beard I'd ever seen, a woman with a moustache and a girl with a bossy face and a mass of black hair.

'Tea?' I heard a voice saying from somewhere deep inside me. 'Even though it's midnight?'

'Do you know of a better time for having tea?' asked Grandad.

'Er . . . teatime?' I said, weakly.

Grandad went out to the hall and the bearded man stepped forwards towards me, grabbed my hand and shook it.

'You must be Keith the Teeth's grandson! He said you'd come to stay.'

The man's hand was soft and hairy. I noticed he was in a Cub leader's uniform, while the woman wore a Brownie leader's jumper.

'I'm Monty Moon, the local Werewolf Cub Pack leader,' he said.

Now the woman came across. 'And I'm Mrs Moon, Millie,' she said. 'I'm Brown Howl.'

And just to prove it, she tipped back her head and let out an enormous howl that shook the kitchen ceiling and turned my legs to jelly.

Chapter 8

I GRIPPED THE SIDE of the worktop, panting like mad. It felt as if I'd just done a hundred-metre dash. I watched as Grandad strode over to the kitchen dresser, uncorked a couple of wine bottles and placed them on the table.

'1998 vintage,' he announced. 'A very good year.' And he began wiping a couple of wine glasses with his hanky.

'I do wish you wouldn't do that, Keith,' said Mrs Moon. 'It's such a disgusting habit! Don't you keep a tea towel in this place?'

While Grandad and Mr and Mrs Moon busied themselves looking for a clean tea towel, I turned towards the door to the hall, determined to make a run for it. But there, blocking my way, was the bossy-faced girl.

'You off already?' she asked, with a sly grin.

'What's it got to do with you?' I snapped back.

'Ooooo . . . get you,' said the girl. She looked hard at me and her grin grew wider. 'You're scared, aren't you?'

'Yes! I mean . . . no!'

'Make your mind up. I'm Scarlet, by the way. That's my great-uncle and aunt.' She jabbed a thumb in the direction of the Werewolf Cub leader and Brown Howl. Grandad was pouring them both glasses of what looked to me suspiciously like blood.

'Cheers!' said Mr and Mrs Moon, raising their glasses.

'Cheers!' said Grandad, knocking his drink back in one go. He looked across the room at me. 'You're a bit on the young and skinny side to be drinking the hard stuff, my boy,' he said, 'but there's a can of tomato juice in the fridge, if you'd like it.'

'I expect he'd like a Coke, like I would,' said Scarlet.

'How you kids can drink that muck, I really don't know,' muttered Mr Moon with a frown. Grandad opened the fridge door and tossed a couple of cans to Scarlet.

She gave one to me. I put it straight down on the worktop.

'You've got to be kidding,' I said.

'Suit yourself,' said Scarlet, with a shrug.

OK. It said Coke on the can, but I wasn't going to be fooled by that. I'd seen what came out of Grandad's so-called wine bottles.

Scarlet was still standing in the doorway. 'You can see you're Keith's grandson,' she said, 'you look just like him.'

'I don't!'

'You do!'

I could feel myself blushing with anger. 'I don't! I mean, look at those teeth of his. I haven't got teeth like that.'

'Oh, those. They're not his real fangs. They're just false ones. He only wears them once a month for full moons and that. You know, he's dead funny, your grandad. He knows some really wicked jokes.' She paused. 'I suppose I'll have to introduce you to the rest of the Fang Gang.'

I stared at her, open-mouthed. 'The what?'

'The Fang Gang. There's a group of us. We've all got relatives who have powers from the dark side. It'll be great to have a new member. We need a bit of new blood.' She nudged me hard in the ribs. 'Get it? New *blood*! It'll certainly give Gory a bit of a shock. He's been getting far too big for his boots lately. If you're not having that Coke, I will.'

Scarlet walked across to the table to get my can. I seized the moment and slipped past her into the hall. I put out my hand to turn the key in the front door. But the key was gone! Desperately, I turned the door handle and pulled. The door held firm.

Then I remembered how Grandad had popped out of the kitchen to the hall. Now I knew why. To take the door key, so I couldn't escape!

I was trapped in the house of a vampire. A vampire who was my grandad.

Chapter 9

THERE WAS ONLY ONE thing left to do. I ran all the way up the stairs, past Grandad's room and his coffin, to my attic bedroom.

Shutting myself in, I jammed the table hard against the door, then jammed the chair hard against the table. I was probably kidding myself, but it made me feel just a little safer.

From the bottom of my bag I took out Mr Chumps.

OK, I know what you're thinking. He's got a teddy bear! Well, let me tell you, Mr Chumps is not a teddy bear. And he's not a pink rabbit, either. I'm not that kind of saddo. Mr Chumps is a tyrannosaurus rex; king of the dinosaurs. He has stegosauruses for break-

fast. And he's *on my side*. I needed people on my side. This is what the line-up looked like:

THEM

Grandad
(vampire)

Mr Moon
(werewolf)

Mrs Moon
(werewolf)

Scarlet
(werewolf + a **GIRL!**)

The Fang Gang
(??? Could be Scarlet's imaginary friends)

ME

Me (definitely
NOT a vampire)

Mr Chumps
(tyrannosaurus rex)

I put Mr Chumps on my pillow and climbed into bed. I didn't put my pyjamas on. That way, I thought, I'd be able to make a really quick getaway at first light. Even with the curtain closed, the moon filled my bedroom with a ghostly glow. I held on tight to Mr Chumps to try to stop myself shaking. I wondered how Mum and Dad were getting on aboard their cruise ship. And I wondered whether Gran would be in bed, or whether she would still be packing her knitting needles away, ready for her spell in prison.

I just wanted to go home. And the tears started welling up in me at the thought that I wouldn't be able to get away from this awful place and these hideous people. At least, not until the morning. Until then, I knew I must not, under any circumstances, let myself fall asleep.

The sounds of laughter, chatter and the occasional howl drifted up the stairs from the kitchen.

All I had to do now was to stay awake until first light. With any luck Grandad would be sleeping off the effects of his midnight tea party and I'd be able to make my getaway.

Although terrible pictures of blood-stained

vampires kept swirling round my mind, it was hard not to feel sleepy. I yawned. Closed my eyes . . . And thought what a dangerous and a busy day I had ahead of me, making my escape from Goolish . . . I'd need all the energy I could get. Perhaps just a short sleep . . . I yawned some more. Perhaps it wouldn't be a bad idea to get . . . some . . . sleep . . .

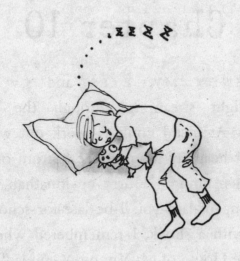

Chapter 10

I OPENED MY EYES and saw the sunlight streaming through the attic window. At first I couldn't work out why I couldn't hear my mum at the bottom of the stairs screaming: 'Hurry-up-Jonathan-you-lazy-lump-of-lard-you'll-be-late-for-school!' Then with a shock, I remembered where I was. The House of My Vampire Grandad!

I slid off the bed, stuffed Mr Chumps into

my bag and pulled the table and chair away from the door. Slinging my bag over my shoulder, I opened the bedroom door and crept down the stairs. Grandad's bedroom door was shut and when I reached the bottom of the stairs, I found the front door was still locked. No problem. If I could get myself up on to the draining board, I could let myself out through the kitchen window.

I pushed open the kitchen door.

'Ah, boy, you're up! I was beginning to think I'd have to come and hammer on your door!'

There, standing at the kitchen table, frying pan in his hand, and wearing a plastic apron with the words 'KING OF THE KITCHEN' written across the front of it was my grandad. He put the frying pan on the cooker and straightaway the smell of sizzling bacon wafted up my nose. My mouth started watering. I was starving. No wonder, I'd not had anything to eat since yesterday teatime at Gran's. I knew I should really try and escape there and then, but I didn't. It was the thought – and the smell – of food that did it. I saw a film once about a plane crash in the jungle where the survivors got so hungry they started eating beetles and spiders. Well, I'm not saying I was hungry enough to tuck into a plate of fried beetles and spiders, but eggs and bacon I could not resist. Even if it meant staying a bit longer in Drac's Cottage.

'Two eggs or three?' asked Grandad.

'Three, please,' I replied, quick as a flash.

'I don't usually have a cooked breakfast. Not when it's just me on my own,' said Grandad. 'But it's not every day your only grandson pays you a visit, is it?'

Grandad smiled and I saw he didn't have fangs any more. (In fact, they were in a glass on the window sill.) He looked very gummy and not at all scary.

'You'll have to excuse the curtains still being drawn, my boy,' Grandad said. 'I'm not a big fan of sunlight. Particularly early on in the morning.'

We had eggs, bacon, tomatoes, mushrooms, fried bread and sausages. I passed on the tomato sauce, though. I wasn't going to take any chances.

'Like another sausage?' asked Grandad.

I nodded. I couldn't speak, owing to my mouth being full.

'Thought you might,' said Grandad, dropping another *two* sausages on my plate. 'They're tasty, eh?' He winked. 'Special recipe.'

Then Grandad suddenly launched into his autobiography, just like a proper grandad.

'Learnt to cook when I was doing National Service in the Army, I did,' he said. 'I even spent some time working as a professional chef.' He shook his head. 'Then Italian food became all the rage and we had to start using garlic. That was the end for me.' He paused, and he suddenly looked worried. 'Er . . . I hope you didn't feel too scared last night.'

'No,' I lied.

'Only it must have been quite something for you to come away from home and stay with some old fellow you'd never met.'

'Quite something' was putting it mildly.

'I expect you noticed I locked the front door,' Grandad went on.

I nodded.

'I didn't want you to take it into your head to go for a midnight stroll or something,' said Grandad. 'I mean, obviously you are fine in the house here with me and the Moons. But these days, you know, you can't be too careful. There are some very weird people out there.'

I gawped.

'Anyway, you'd better have this.' Grandad pressed a door key into my hand. 'Then if you need to let yourself in, you can. It's good to have you here, boy. Though of course, I was sorry to hear about your gran being sent down.' Suddenly, Grandad laughed. 'Here, I shouldn't tell you this, I know. It's wicked. But, what do you get if you cross a granny with a chicken?'

I shook my head.

'*Granbled* eggs!' chortled Grandad. He tipped back his head till I could see all his gums and started roaring with laughter. I joined in. I couldn't help it, even though the joke was terrible. As we laughed, I became aware of someone hammering at the front door.

Grandad must have heard it too, because he suddenly stopped laughing.

'Strike a stake through my heart, is it that time already? That'll be Millie and Scarlet at the door, come to give you a lift to school, my boy,' said Grandad.

Give me a lift to **WHERE?**

Chapter 11

I COULDN'T BELIEVE IT! Grandad had arranged for me to go to *school*! I already had a good idea about what sort of school it would be, a school for freaks and weirdoes.

As for Great-aunt Millie, the moustache she'd been wearing last night seemed to have gone. When I looked closely at her in the rear-view mirror, though, I could still

see a trace of it underneath her nose.

'Goolish School's not bad as schools go,' Scarlet said, 'not that I've ever been to any other schools.'

I let Scarlet rabbit on while I looked out of the window and got my first glimpses of Goolish by day. It was sort of stacked up on a steep hill. On top of the hill and right round the edges, were the woods I'd driven through in the taxi the night before. At the bottom of the hill was the sea. I couldn't see any boats though.

'You won't see any boats,' said Scarlet, as if reading my mind. 'The beach is too steep and there are lots of dangerous rocks out in the bay. There have been hundreds of shipwrecks over the years. That's why we've got so many ghosts staying here.'

I was still trying to work out just what Scarlet had meant by her last comment, when the car screeched to a halt.

'Get a move on, you guys,' said Great-aunt Millie. 'Or you'll be getting a late mark in the register.'

We clambered out.

'Scarlet! Your maths homework! Honestly, you'd forget your head if it wasn't screwed on,' yelled Great-aunt Millie.

Scarlet took me into the classroom. It didn't look a lot different to the one back home. As she dumped her bag on a chair a tall, dark girl sidled up behind her. She had deep, piercing eyes which she fixed on me.

Scarlet turned around. 'Oh, hi, Griselda,' she said. 'This is Jonathan. Mr Leech's grandson?'

'Hi,' said Griselda, without smiling.

'Griselda's in the Fang Gang too,' Scarlet said.

For a moment, I thought Griselda must have a twitch or something, because her eye kept flickering. Then I realised she was winking at Scarlet.

'You stay here, Jonathan,' said Scarlet, following Griselda to the door. 'I've just got to go and er . . . brush my hair.'

A likely story, I thought. You'd need a yard broom to get to grips with Scarlet's mass of hair. No, she and Griselda were obviously off to the girls' toilet to have a girlie-type chat.

I plonked myself down next to Scarlet's bag. No sooner had I got my feet under the table when the chair was pulled out from behind me and I landed on the floor.

I looked up into the face of an enormous

guy with a scowl and thick, dark eyebrows.

'You! Get your bottom off my chair,' he threatened. Only he didn't use the word 'bottom'.

'Thanks to you, it is off your chair, stupid,' I replied, getting up.

I stood facing him. He grabbed the front of my sweatshirt. I was about to give his shins a good kicking when a voice shouted from the doorway:

'Gory! Sit down this instant!'

Gory sat down that instant.

I turned round and found myself facing the class teacher. She took my name and then directed me to a spare chair next to a girl with frizzy blonde hair at the front of the class.

'Tiffany will look after you,' said the teacher. 'She's new to the school too. And as for you, Gory,' she eyeballed the tall guy who was now sitting down, sulking. 'You can stay in at break time.'

'Hi,' Tiffany said to me with a smile. She was one of those girls who specialise in soppy looks. 'You don't want to take any notice of Gory. He's just a big bully.'

I had half a mind to point out to her that it's tricky not to take notice of someone who's grabbed you by the throat, but I didn't. I just gave her a quick smile back and hoped it wasn't too soppy.

Scarlet and Griselda came in and sat down with Gory at the back of the class.

At break time, Scarlet and Griselda came haring over to me as soon as we got out into the playground.

'What have you done to Gory?' Griselda demanded.

'Nothing – yet,' I replied. 'The teacher came in, just as I was about to give him a good thumping –'

'You got him into trouble,' said Scarlet.

'He pulled me off my chair!' I protested.

'It's dead against the rules of the Fang Gang to get another member into trouble,' said Griselda, glowering at me.

'I'm not in your stupid Fang Gang,' I said. 'And I don't want to be in your Fang Gang, especially if it has dumb gorillas like Gory in it.'

'Oh, let him get on with it,' said Griselda, marching off.

But Scarlet stood there looking at me. 'Sorry about Gory,' she said. 'It's just that he's got a bit of a quick temper. I'll get him to make it up with you at lunchtime.' And off

she went to find Griselda to have another
girlie-type talk.

Back in class, Tiffany passed me a note:

Don't worry about Gory and his mates. I
know a place in the playground where it's
safe from the likes of them. Stick with me.
Tiffany.

*OK, so Tiffany may be the soppiest girl in
Goolish*, I thought, *but she's got one thing going
for her: she's not a werewolf.*

Chapter 12

Tiffany's 'safe place' turned out to be a corner of the playground directly under the head teacher's office window. It was not somewhere you'd choose to hang out, not if you were cool, but I had no choice.

Tiffany asked me how I came to be living in Goolish and I told her I was staying with my grandad.

'That must be nice.'

I thought about the cooked breakfast and Grandad's terrible jokes. 'Yeh, it is.' But I didn't tell her where he lived or about any of the weird stuff that had happened since I'd been here.

'I moved here during the summer holidays, with my mum,' said Tiffany. 'She wanted to move out of the city and the houses here are dead cheap. My mum's an investigative journalist.'

'Wow.'

'She's *always* on the telly.'

'Yeh?'

'Yeh.'

Amazing. I'd never met anyone who'd been on the telly.

'Do you like living in Goolish?' I asked Tiffany. It sounded a bit of a dumb question, but I mean what sort of thing can you say to someone you don't know very well, particularly a girl?

'It's all right,' said Tiffany. 'We've got a

massive house . . .' She looked around and lowered her voice. 'But –'

'But what?'

'There's something very odd about the place. And I've got a theory –'

I didn't get a chance to find out what Tiffany's theory was, because at that moment I looked up and saw Scarlet standing there.

'We'll see you later, then, Jonathan,' said Scarlet.

Not if I see you first, I thought.

As soon as the bell went for home time, the class charged out through the door like a herd of stampeding wildebeest. I hung back, tidying my drawer, writing my name on my new draft book, English book, maths book . . . When the last voice had disappeared, and it was quiet enough to hear the fluorescent light tube buzzing above my head, I crept out of school.

There was only one way to go: the way that Gory would not expect me to go. Away from the churchyard and Drac's Cottage. A couple

of minutes later, I found myself on the seafront. I crossed the road and leaned over the railings, looking down at the rocky beach.

'Just you and me now, eh?' sneered a voice.

I turned and there, suddenly in front of me, was Gory. Where he'd come from I couldn't work out. It was like he'd appeared out of thin air.

He strode towards me, his fists clenched.

Behind him, I saw Griselda and Scarlet, running across the road towards us.

'Wrong again,' I said. 'It's just you and two girls –'

'Gory!' yelled Scarlet.

As Gory looked round, I turned on my heel and ran.

Both Gory and Griselda were bigger and stronger than me. Where I was heading I didn't know, except that it was away from the Fang Gang. But the seafront was straight and flat. My legs and arms seemed to know how to move in rhythm. I felt the wind blowing through my hair and pricking my eyes until they watered – just like when you ride a bike downhill fast. I was breathing easily and comfortably.

When I glanced towards the road I was amazed to see that I was going faster than all the cars and lorries. It was brilliant! I pushed harder with my legs and found myself spurting away even faster. Out of the corner of my eye I glimpsed startled expressions on peoples' faces as I flashed by.

I reached the end of the seafront and had to cross the road, but the lights were against me! I hit the button and stood running on the spot, desperate to keep the amazing rhythm going so that I could leave the Fang Gang dead in their tracks. They were still some way off, back along the seafront, but they were closing in on me fast.

The lights changed and I stepped into the road, just missing a lorry that had jumped the lights. I pushed with my legs to get my power run going again. Nothing happened. Suddenly, I felt wobbly and breathless. My arms and legs wouldn't work together and I could feel a stitch coming on. I glanced over my shoulder. Behind me, Gory was within shouting – or rather swearing – distance. My chest was thumping like a hammer. I hardly seemed to know how to put one foot in front of the other. I stopped and bent almost double, gasping for breath. I could hear the racing footsteps closing in.

Gory and the Fang Gang had me now.

Chapter 13

'**J**ONATHAN?' enquired a small voice. I raised my head and saw Tiffany frowning at me. 'Quick, jump in,' she ordered, opening the passenger door of a silver cabriolet. I didn't need asking twice. Tiffany tumbled in after me. A woman with smart blonde hair and shades sat behind the wheel. 'Mum,' said Tiffany, 'this is Jonathan, and he's coming home for tea.'

Tiffany's mum turned round, took off her shades and studied me. It was amazing. Although she'd been on telly loads of times, she didn't look much different to my mum, except of course, she was younger.

'Oh, poppet, you've managed to make a little friend, at last!' she gushed to Tiffany.

'Not now, Mum,' said Tiffany. 'Just drive!'

We shot away from the kerb just as Gory drew level with the car. I couldn't resist giving him a smile and small, regal wave.

Tiffany had been right about her house. It *was* massive. We had to put carrier bags on our feet so that we didn't get the carpets grubby and then we went into the sitting room. There, on top of the 150 cm wide plasma telly, were hundreds of pictures of Tiffany's mum.

'I am an investigative journalist, Jonathan. I do a lot of exposés. Do you know what exposés are?'

Before I could answer, Tiffany's mum went on, 'It means I expose anything that's bad.

Anything antisocial. Anything that's er . . . not very nice. Now, you'd better ring your mother and let her know where you are.'

'He lives with his grandad,' said Tiffany.

Tiffany's mum handed me a pink mobile. I dialled and heard Grandad's voice:

'Drac's Cottage?'

I prayed that neither Tiffany nor her mum had heard.

'Hi, Grandad. It's Jonathan. I'm at Tiffany's. See ya later.'

Tea wasn't up to much. Hardly surprising really, you could tell just by looking at them that Tiffany and her mum weren't the sort of people who enjoy their food. In fact, I suppose I was lucky to get what I did, which was: a glass of water and a plate of salad. I left half of it, just in case I started turning into a rabbit.

After tea we watched telly. And the telly we watched was a DVD of Tiffany's mum's exposés. We saw her exposing a supermarket chain selling baked beans that were only half baked. We saw her exposing a company making toy Daleks that went 'Mama! Mama!' instead of 'Exterminate! Exterminate!'

'I'd better be getting back to Grandad's,' I

said as another exposé was about to hit the screen. I was starving. I hoped Grandad was cooking up something good for supper. With a bit of luck, he might have bought some more of the sausages we'd had for breakfast.

'Then we'll drive you home,' said Tiffany's mum. 'I don't think you should walk home alone through Goolish. There are some seriously weird people in this town.'

As we sped through the town centre, I could feel my stomach rumbling. I thought again of Grandad and the fantastic breakfast I'd had with him. I remembered what happens if you cross a granny with a chicken and laughed inside myself. If only he wasn't a vampire. *Perhaps*, I thought, *he could be persuaded to give it up*. He must be well past vampire retirement age, after all. If he gave up vampiring, he'd be a really cool, ordinary grandad. He'd take me swimming and I'd be able to have friends back to play. He'd get satellite telly. And I wouldn't be hounded by Scarlet and her stupid Fang Gang. I made a decision: it was up to me to get Grandad to give up vampiring.

I peered out into the darkness. The street lights had come on. They weren't like the street lights at home. They seemed to give off a sort of eerie, yellowish glow and made you feel really gloomy. Nobody spoke and when we pulled up at some traffic lights Tiffany's Mum put a CD on to cover up the silence. It was called *Sing-along to the World's 20 Soppiest Lurv Songs With Shane Crush*.

'*I thought our love was strong and tr-u-e*

Bound together as if by supergl-u-e . . .' sang Tiffany and her mum.

Then, suddenly, 'Aaaaaargh!' they screamed.

At first I thought it was just part of the song. But I quickly realised I was wrong. These weren't soppy screams. These were screams of terror and fear. I looked up and saw that they were staring out of the windscreen. And on the other side of the windscreen was a face. An old, pale face with piercing eyes and two

long, sharp fangs. A face that leered and
grinned with menace. A face I recognised.

Grandad's face.

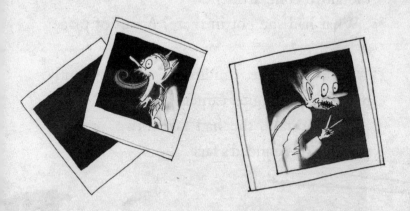

Chapter 14

GRANDAD MOVED ROUND from the windscreen to the driver's window, still leering, still grinning, but now clawing at the window with his long, bony fingers. I slithered down on to the floor of the car. This was bad enough, but I knew it would be even worse if Grandad saw me and started yelling my name.

Tiffany and her mum had stopped screaming.

Peering through the front seats, I watched Tiffany's mum rummage frantically through the glove compartment.

What had she got in there? A can of mace? A revolver?

'Ye-e-es!' she muttered, triumphantly pulling out a digital camera.

In an instant, she had taken two or three pictures of Grandad's face.

'Gotcha!' she shouted.

'Quick, Mum, the lights have changed!' yelled Tiffany.

Off we roared with a screech of tyres. We didn't stop until we'd gone through another three sets of lights (two red, one green) and had reached the seafront. Tiffany's mum parked up under a dull street light and we all sat there for a moment, watching the dark waves roll up the beach. Tiffany's mum turned round to me and said:

'Are you OK, Jonathan?'

I nodded.

'What a horrid old man,' said Tiffany's mum.

'Gross,' Tiffany agreed.

'I think he was one of those old age pensioner hoodies,' Tiffany's mum went on. 'There's a piece about them on the front page of the paper.'

Tiffany's mum pointed to a folded newspaper on the back seat next to me. I picked it up and opened it to see the front page:

DAILY WAIL

Supermarket Serial Psycho Shopper (63) Back in Court!

On other pages: We say: time to get tough with these old r-age pensioners! Boot the Pensioner Yobbos out of our shopping centres!

'If you ask me they should lock the lot of them up and throw away the key,' Tiffany's mum went on. 'Still, I've got our picture of him. I've got all the evidence the police need.'

'Er, actually, you haven't got a picture of him,' said Tiffany. She was going through the programs on the digital camera. 'There are three very nice pictures of the car window, but none of the old man's face.' She paused and then added in a sinister whisper, 'And that can mean only one thing, can't it?'

'Yes, the stupid camera's bust!' fumed Tiffany's mum. 'Now, where did you say your grandad's house was, Jonathan?'

'Er . . . right here!' I said, quickly. There was no way I was going to let them know that Grandad lived in Drac's Cottage.

Tiffany's mum peered through the passenger window. 'You live *here*?' she asked, with a gasp.

I looked out of the window and saw we had pulled up in front of a small shop. The sign above the window read:

Veronica Vickers Beautiful Knickers

And the window display was full of knickers, bras and pants.

'Er . . . well, when I say *here*,' I began, 'I mean just round the –'

But before I could finish, Tiffany's mum uttered an excited yell and leapt out of the car. She trotted across the pavement and peered at the bargains in Veronica Vickers' window.

'. . . Er . . . I live just round the corner,' I explained for Tiffany's benefit.

I needn't have bothered. She wasn't listening. She was still busy with the digital camera. She turned excitedly to me.

'At last! I've got the proof!' she said. 'Do you want to know the real reason those pictures of that disgusting old man didn't come out?'

I opened my mouth to speak, but I didn't get a chance to answer. Tiffany had started and she was going to finish.

'The camera is working fine. If it wasn't, there wouldn't have been any pictures at all. It was just the old man who was missing. Now, we know what kind of people don't have reflections? Whose faces can't be caught on camera?'

'Do we?' I answered.

'Of course! Vampires! Honestly, don't you know anything? That disgusting old man was a vampire! Don't you see, it all makes sense! I knew there was something weird about this town. And Gory, Scarlet and the rest of them in the Fang Gang, they're all part of it. I've tried telling Mum, but she won't listen. But you and me, Jonathan, we're going to put a stop to their disgusting practices. Right? I've read all about it on the Internet. I'm going to be a vampire slayer, just like Buffy. Buffy had a helper called Angel.'

She paused. I knew, I just *knew* what was coming next.

'Will you be my Angel, Jonathan?'

I didn't open my mouth, for fear I'd throw up with the horrible yuckiness of it all. Luckily, just at that moment, Tiffany's mum came back from her spot of window shopping.

'Tiffany, poppet, Jonathan is trying to get out of the car.'

You bet I was. Tiffany got out and tipped her seat forward to let me out.

'Now you're sure you're OK walking home from here?' asked Tiffany's mum with a frown. 'I simply couldn't bear the thought of you suddenly coming face-to-face with that horrid old man.'

'I'll be fine. Honest,' I replied, secretly wondering just what I'd say to that 'horrid old man' when I saw him.

I stepped out on to the pavement. Tiffany gave me a sly wink.

'See you Monday . . . *Angel*,' she whispered, as she stepped back into her mum's car.

Chapter 15

I T WAS REALLY DARK NOW, but the moon gave just enough light for me to make out the shadowy outline of the church on top of the hill. If I headed that way I knew I wouldn't be far from Drac's Cottage. I hoped that Gory and the rest of the Fang Gang were too busy doing whatever it was they did after dark, to be bothered with trying to hunt me down.

As I began to leave the centre of town, the streets got narrower, steeper and darker. All the time I was thinking about Grandad. Why did he have to go around being a vampire and scaring people at traffic lights? It was one thing having a gran in prison, that was quite cool in its way. I mean, I could imagine showing the newspaper article that Tiffany's mum had to people in my class and saying:

'That's my gran. She's doing time for trolley rage. So, don't mess with me. OK?'

But a grandad who was a vampire? That was just so gross and embarrassing. The frustrating thing was, I felt if I could only get him to give up vampiring, he'd be a really great grandad.

Halfway up the hill, I reckoned I must be getting closer to Drac's Cottage, but just how close I had no idea. With a growing sense of dread, I realised I was lost.

The road levelled out briefly and I saw I was standing in front of a garage. A flickering sign read:

MORT'S MOTORS
MINIBUSES
Body Repair Workshop

A yellow light shone through the glass in the large garage doors. I went up to them and saw that they were ajar. I pushed them open a little and stepped inside.

The garage seemed to be full of old hearses. An extremely pale, thin man with sunken cheeks stood in front of them. He looked hard at me. Twenty-four hours ago, I would have found him terrifying and scary. But after what I had been through recently, he seemed to be the regular sort of creepy guy you got in this part of town.

'I'm looking for Drac's Cottage,' I said.

'Well, you won't find it in here,' he sighed. 'I guess you must be Keith the Teeth's grandson. Am I right, or am I right?'

I nodded.

'I'm Mort,' the man said, sadly. 'You'll find your grandad's place straight up the hill, second lane on the left. His cottage is third on the right. And by the way, if you ever need taking anywhere, I'm your man.'

A thought struck me, something that might serve as a back-up plan, should my mission to

get Grandad to give up being a vampire go horribly wrong. 'What time's the next mini-bus?' I asked.

'Five minutes to midnight,' said Mort. 'Churchyard Express.'

'I mean – out of Goolish.'

'Out of Goolish?' said Mort, with a frown. 'I might be running one Wednesday week.' he paused. 'But then again, I might not.'

That was it, then. If I was going to have to stay in Goolish till Wednesday week at least, my mission to turn Grandad into a normal human being just *had* to succeed.

I stumbled up the hill towards Drac's Cottage. What had Mort said? Third street on the left or fourth street on the right? Clouds now covered the moon. I took the fourth on the right and immediately crashed into a large skip. I rubbed my shin. It throbbed like mad where I had grazed it. I turned around, went down the hill and turned left into a lane which felt familiar, even in the gloomy darkness.

I found Drac's Cottage unlit. Surprised? Not. I tried the front door. It wasn't locked.

I went in and switched on the hall light. I hoped against hope to hear the sizzling frying pan and to catch the smell of cooking sausages. But there was nothing. The whole cottage was still and quiet.

On the kitchen worktop, I saw a note propped up against a ketchup bottle:

Dear Boy
GONE TO SEE SOME
BODY
Grandad

I pulled open the fridge door. Not a sausage. I looked on the window sill. Just as I'd thought – no fangs in the glass.

Angry, tired and hungry, I traipsed up the narrow, wooden staircase to my bedroom. I sat on the bed and clutched Mr Chumps for comfort. Then I chucked him on to the floor. I didn't need comfort! I needed a plan of action! A plan of action to stop Grandad being a vampire. I took my pen and notebook and lay down on the bed.

Chapter 16

WAYS OF STOPPING GRANDAD
BEING A VAMPIRE:

A: Drive a stake through his heart.

Problems with this method:

1: I haven't got a stake.

2: I haven't got a hammer

3: Grandad would end up a blob

4: If Grandad was a blob he wouldn't be able to take me swimming or buy me pizza.

B: ??????

How long I dozed off for I don't know. When I woke up it was still night-time but the clouds had gone and my room was filled with moonlight. My shin was throbbing from when I'd knocked it crashing into the skip. It was the same shin I'd bruised on Grandad's coffin the day before. Skip . . . Coffin . . . Skip . . . a plan of action began to form in my brain! If I was to get Grandad to give up being a vampire, the first thing to do, surely, was to get rid of all his vampiring gear!

I crept downstairs to the kitchen, found a black plastic sack under the sink and filled it with anything that looked like a bottle of blood. It was a pity that the wine glass was empty, but the fangs would surely be back in the morning. I could deal with them then.

I took the bag out to hall, left it by the front door and went back up the stairs to Grandad's room. The door was ajar and I pushed it fully open. There, covered in moonlight, was Grandad's coffin. It cast strange shadows on the walls and ceiling.

Upright, against the nearest wall, stood the coffin's lid. I lifted it up and carefully placed it on top of the coffin. There was a satisfying clunk as it slipped into place. In Grandad's chest of drawers, along with a pair of braces, half a packet of toffees and an electric tooth-brush, I found six screws and a screwdriver. I screwed down the coffin lid. All the time I was listening for the front door, just in case Grandad came home.

Now came the tricky bit. How could I drag a six-foot coffin out of the cottage, up the hill and on to the skip? I bent down and lifted it up from the front. It was surprisingly light, almost as if it was made from balsa wood. I walked it to the landing, then slid it down the stairs to the hall. Then, picking up the black sack with one hand and heaving the coffin up on to my back with the other, I slipped out of the cottage.

Out in the lane it was frosty. I shivered, then started with alarm as I heard a sound that could have been a laugh or a scream coming from the far end of the lane. Supposing I was to meet Grandad now? What would I say? What would I do? I heard the sound again, nearer, above my head. I looked up, just in time to see a screech owl swoop away into the woods.

I didn't want to spend any more time doing this than was strictly necessary. I began to run. Straight up the hill, round the corner to the skip. I chucked the black sack in. Then I backed up to the end of the skip and, in one speedy movement, let go of the coffin, spun round and pushed it into the skip. There came a crash that echoed around the night. Dogs began to howl. But when I peered into the skip, I saw the coffin was still intact.

I crept away back to Drac's Cottage. I locked the front door with the key Grandad had given me. I climbed into bed and snuggled down, taking Mr Chumps with me. I felt warm and happy inside. Tomorrow, things would be better. Tomorrow, things would be different. Tomorrow, I would have a real grandad.

Chapter 17

I WOKE TO FIND BRIGHT morning sunlight streaming into my eyes. I walked across to the window and looked out. Tumbling down to the seafront, the houses of Goolish looked friendly and inviting. In the distance, the waves were dancing on the sea. It looked a fairly ordinary sort of seaside town.

I opened my bedroom door and listened. I

couldn't hear Grandad. I wondered what time he had come in; if he had gone up to his bedroom and found his coffin missing or if he had gone straight to the kitchen.

There was no sign of him in his bedroom. Just a mark on the carpet where the coffin had been. There was no sign of him in the front room or in the kitchen either. His note was still on the worktop; his false fangs' glass still empty.

I decided to go back to my room. I was halfway up the stairs when suddenly there came the sound of furious knocking on the front door. I froze. I could hear giggling voices too. Voices I recognised: the Fang Gang! But I was safe, I knew. The front door was locked and only Grandad and I had keys.

The giggling stopped. I peered down the stairs. By the front door was a shimmering, eerie light. The light began to take on a shape. And the shape it took on was Gory's!

I stuffed my fist into my mouth to stop my teeth from chattering. I backed away into the corner of the landing. I peered over the banister and could just see Gory, though he'd obviously not seen me. He looked as scared as I was. He started to walk forward, tripped over the doormat, knocked over the vase of dying flowers and started swearing like mad.

He picked himself up and went through to the front room. I heard a squeak of the window latch and then the voices of the others squealing with excitement as they climbed through the window into the cottage.

They came through to the hall and I pulled back away from the banister.

'Mr Leech?' called Griselda. 'It's only us!'

I heard them go through to the kitchen.

I looked down the stairs to the hall – and gasped in amazement. There on the bottom step stood two figures looking up at me: a black kid with a stony face and a little lad so small, I wondered they'd let him out of play-group.

'Mummy!' he screamed, before I'd even had time to panic.

Gory, Griselda and Scarlet rushed back into the hall.

'Alfie, shhh!' said Griselda to the little boy. He stood pointing up at me. Too late, I started clambering up the stairs to my room. Straightaway, they all started charging up after me. This time, I knew, they had me cornered.

This time there would be no escape.

Chapter 18

'WHAT'S THIS? asked Gory, picking up Mr Chumps by his tail and swinging him round his head.

'You can see what it is. It's a tyrannosaurus rex,' replied Griselda.

All five of them, Gory, Griselda, Scarlet, the black kid and the little one were sitting with me on the floor in my bedroom.

'Put it back on the bed, sit down and shut up,' said Scarlet.

Gory put Mr Chumps back on the bed, sat down and shut up. Scarlet may not have been the eldest or the biggest, but she was obviously in charge. She took out her English draft book and opened it up. I peered across to see what she had written.

Emergency Meeting of the Fang Gang
Agenda
1: Apologies
2: Applications for membership: 1: Jonathan
3: TIFFANY BLISS!!!!!!
4: Any Other Business

'As we're all here, I declare this emergency meeting of the Fang Gang open,' said Scarlet, before I had time to even open my mouth. 'Item 1: Apologies. That means Gory and Jonathan apologising to each other for being such a pair of idiots.'

'But he was sitting on my chair!' Gory protested.

'You pulled me off it!' I replied.

'Honestly. Boys!' said Griselda with a sigh.

Scarlet glowered at Gory.

'Oh, all right . . .' muttered Gory. 'Sorry.'

'Er . . . yeh . . . that's all right. Er . . . sorry,' I mumbled, half-heartedly. 'Now would you all mind leaving my grandad's house?'

'Sit down and shut up,' said Scarlet in the same tone of voice she'd used on Gory. 'Item 2: Jonathan's application for membership.'

'Hang on a moment, I haven't applied for anything —' I began, but Scarlet ignored me.

'Griselda will fill you in on all the background,' said Scarlet. 'She's good at all this stuff. She's even done school projects on it.'

'Right,' said Griselda. 'As you've probably worked out by now, Jonathan, people from the dark side have lived here in Goolish for years. They've come from all over the world. Vampires and werewolves from Europe, zombies from the Caribbean, mummies from the Middle East. Everyone in the Fang Gang is a kid from the dark side. You see, when you get to the age of about ten or so, you begin to develop your special powers.' Griselda paused and smiled at Gory. 'Gory is a ghoul. He's just developing the power of passing through solid objects.' She smiled. 'That walking through the front door just now was really fab, Gory!'

Gory blushed, but being a ghoul it was a very pale sort of blush.

'Crombie,' Griselda turned to the black kid, 'is obviously a zombie.'

'Yeh,' said Crombie, without apparently moving his lips.

'He doesn't say a lot but when he does you'd be well advised to listen to him.'

'Yeh,' said Crombie.

'Little Alfie . . .' Here the little boy who'd blown my cover beamed. 'Well, he's far too young to be in the Fang Gang, really. But he's my next-door neighbour's kid and I usually get lumbered with looking after him. Scarlet, of course, is a young werewolf. She can't do the full transformation bit yet, but her howl is pretty convincing.' Scarlet tipped back her head and howled – like we needed proof.

'And Griselda can turn into a bat!' said Little Alfie, unable to control his excitement.

'Just about,' said Griselda, with a giggle. 'Yeh, I'm a young vampire just like you, Jonathan.'

'Oh, no,' I said. 'You've got it all wrong. I'm not a vampire.' I gave them a wide smile to show them my teeth. 'See? No Fang. No Gang. Sorry.'

I started to get up, but was pulled down again by Scarlet and Griselda.

'Who are you kidding?' snapped Griselda. 'We were all there on the seafront yesterday when you sped off. Only someone with the superhuman strength of a young vampire could have made a power run like that.'

I shook my head. I didn't believe it. I didn't want to believe it. There had to be another

explanation, *any* other explanation. But I couldn't think of one. Then I remembered the Princes and my sudden ability to make telling runs down the football pitch. But that didn't mean I wanted to be friends with this bunch of weirdoes.

'We need you in the Fang Gang,' said Scarlet, quietly.

I snorted. Gory snorted.

Scarlet raised her hand. 'All those in favour of Jonathan joining the Fang Gang,' she said.

Griselda, Crombie the Zombie and Little Alfie raised their hands.

Gory didn't. He pointed at Little Alfie. 'He's too young to vote,' he grumbled.

'Mummy . . . !' wailed Little Alfie.

'Sssh!' said Griselda, clamping a hand over Little Alfie's mouth. 'Let him vote, Gory.'

'All those against?' said Scarlet.

Gory's hand shot up. 'How do we know we can trust him?' he said, with a sideways glance at me.

'He's one of us, isn't he?' replied Scarlet.

'Don't I have a say in all this?' I asked, angrily.

'No!' said Scarlet and Griselda together.

'Supposing I don't want to be in the Fang Gang?' I said.

'Then you'll be on your own,' said Scarlet.

'Suits me,' I replied.

'There are some very weird people out there,' said Griselda.

'The ones in here are hardly normal,' I retorted.

'I don't see why we should have him in the Fang Gang, anyway,' said Gory. 'At least, not until we know just what he might have said to Tiffany Bliss.'

'I've not said anything to Tiffany Bliss!' I yelled.

'We saw you in her mum's car!'

'Is that a crime?'

'Perhaps we'd better put Jonathan in the picture about Tiffany Bliss, then,' said Scarlet.

Chapter 19

'THERE HAVE ALWAYS been people from the light side as well as the dark side living in Goolish.' said Griselda. 'You saw that at school. Obviously not everyone in our class is a young ghoul or vampire like you. And for years everyone's got on fine. The thing is, folk from the dark side aren't that bad; after all, some of the things so-called 'ordinary' people get up to are pretty gruesome too. Like m—'

'Morris dancing?' suggested Crombie, gloomily.

'I was thinking more like murder,' said Griselda, 'or war.'

'Take vampires,' said Scarlet. 'Ever since Bram Stoker wrote *Dracula*, vampires have had a very unfair press. OK, they might enjoy the odd drop of blood now and again, but they don't go around biting people – that is

so medieval. And all that stuff about turning people into vampires by biting them is a load of nonsense. Vampires are born, not made. It's a family thing.' Scarlet looked pointedly at me. 'As you well know, Jonathan.'

'But now Tiffany Bliss and her mum have moved to Goolish,' said Griselda. 'Tiffany doesn't get on with the light-side kids – they get fed up with her going on about the famous TV celebs she's met. And she hates the Fang Gang, because we're different. Of course, she doesn't know it's because we're from the dark side.'

That's how much you know, I thought.

'If she ever found out, of course, that would mean real trouble for all of us. She'd spy on us, watch our every move, get us into trouble.' She paused. 'Even get us and our families moved out of Goolish.'

'Have you told her about us, Jonathan?' snarled Gory. 'About the dark side of Goolish?'

'I didn't tell her anything! What was there

to tell her? I didn't know any of this stuff until you lot told me just now!'

'You seemed very friendly,' said Gory, 'jumping into her car and that.'

'I was trying to get away from you lot!' I protested.

'Only the guilty run,' said Gory. 'I rest my case.'

'He said he didn't say anything. And I for one think we ought to believe him, OK?' said Scarlet. 'Now, any other business? No?'

'Good, then you can go now,' I muttered, standing up.

'Yeh,' said Crombie the Zombie, suddenly.

Five pairs of eyes turned to Crombie.

'There is any other business. Old Mr Leech is missing.'

Two hands – Griselda's on the left, Scarlet's on the right – hauled me down on to the floor again.

And five pairs of eyes turned from Crombie to me.

'What are you staring at me for?' I said. 'I

don't know where he's gone.'

Five pairs of eyes stayed fixed on me.

'Look,' I went on. 'I came home, found this note on the kitchen worktop: "Gone To See Some Body". And then . . . I went up to my room.'

Suddenly, I began to feel really worried about Grandad. I thought of the mean and determined look in Mrs Bliss's eye. I thought of the mean and determined look in Tiffany's eye. Supposing they'd been out late and had seen Grandad? It would've been two against one old man. I wasn't sure what Mrs Bliss wanted done with him, but I bet Tiffany knew where to get hold of a stake and a hammer too.

'You look panicked,' said Scarlet.

'I don't.'

'You do. And only the guilty look panicked,' said Gory.

So I told them about Grandad putting the frighteners on Mrs B and Tiffany at the traffic lights.

'Honestly, old people! They put us all in danger just so they can have a bit of a laugh,' complained Griselda.

'Bet it was funny though, seeing Tiffany and her mum scared like that,' chuckled Little Alfie.

I nodded.

'Never mind that,' said Scarlet, 'the thing is, your grandad came round last night. Well, he had a little too much to drink – as usual – so Uncle Monty brought him back here in the car. There's no way Mrs Bliss or Twitty Tiffany could have seen him. Uncle Monty said he helped him upstairs to his room where he toppled straight into his coffin and fell fast asleep.'

I felt my blood run cold.

'You know how he hates the sunlight,' said Gory, getting up. 'He'll still be in his coffin. I'll go and wake him up.'

'You can't go in his room!' I cried in alarm.

'Wanna bet?' replied Gory. And he was out of the door like a shot.

The others followed and, with a feeling of dread in my stomach, I followed downstairs after them.

'He's not here,' Griselda said.

'Nor is his coffin,' chimed in Crombie, helpfully. 'I think if we can find the coffin, we can find Mr Leech.'

'Jonathan,' said Scarlet, quietly. 'Where is your grandad's coffin?'

Chapter 20

I CHARGED UP THE HILL, the rest of the Fang Gang chasing after me. I was just turning into the lane where the skip was, when a huge lorry shot out and thundered its way up the hill. On the back of the lorry was the skip. In the skip you could see the top of Grandad's coffin sticking out.

'How did that get there?' asked Scarlet, in a horrified voice.

The Fang Gang all turned to look at me.

'I didn't know Grandad was in it!' I blubbered. 'It wasn't heavy at all —'

'Come on, it must've weighed a ton,' said Griselda. 'I can't see how you could have managed to even lift it —'

'He's a young vampire with superhuman powers of strength, isn't he?' pointed out Gory, grimly.

'Don't just stand there, get after it!' yelled Scarlet at me.

'Me?'

'Well, you're the one who can power run!'

I put my head down and charged up the hill. The skip lorry was just in sight. At first I couldn't seem to find the right rhythm, but as the road levelled out at the top of the hill, I really began to get into my stride.

Up the hill I stormed, closing in on the skip lorry with every second. By the time we were out of Goolish and on to the flat, open hillside, I was close enough to read the lorry's number plate. Then I began to feel my legs go – I couldn't last out much longer. With one final bound I lurched forward towards the chain dangling from the back of the lorry. I grabbed at it, heaved myself aboard and held on tightly.

After a bit, we turned off the road and went down the hillside into a small valley. I peered round the side of the skip lorry and saw that we were at the council dump. For a second, the thought crossed my mind that I had finally escaped from Goolish! I could leap off the lorry, get myself back on to the main road and keep going until I came to the first town. But the next second I looked up and saw the top of the coffin sticking out of the skip. No, I couldn't run off now. The man in the coffin might be a vampire, but he was my grandad.

As soon as the skip stopped, I jumped off, ran up to the cab and hammered on the driver's door.

'You've got to stop!' I yelled. 'My grandad's in that skip!'

The driver wound down his window and

glowered down at me. I didn't like the look of him one bit. He had a bald head, beady eyes and a fat neck. When Griselda had mentioned that ordinary human beings get up to some pretty dreadful stuff like murder, this was the kind of guy she had in mind.

'Get out of it!' he shouted at me. 'Do you hear me? Or do you want me to drop this skip on your head?'

I didn't know what to do. I suppose I could have said: 'Now look here, Baldy, I'm a vampire, see, and if you don't let me rescue my grandad from that coffin, I'll do something to you that won't be very nice at all!' But I wasn't sure what it was I could do. After all, according to Griselda, twenty-first-century vampires didn't go in for all that biting stuff.

Baldy revved his engine. Just then, I heard a car hooting behind me. I turned round and saw Mort driving one of his ancient hearses at speed. It braked fiercely and went into a spin. It was still in a spin when the rear door flew upwards and out tumbled Gory, Scarlet, Griselda, Crombie the Zombie and Little Alfie.

'Don't worry, Jonathan, we'll save him!' yelled Scarlet. 'Gory, scare the lorry driver so he runs off! Then we can get Mr Leech and his coffin!'

'No sweat,' said Gory, clenching his fists. Soon, he faded into the pale ghoul I'd seen walking through Grandad's door. Whizzing through the air at the speed of light, he sailed straight towards the first lorry he saw. The petrified driver lost control and crashed into a mountain of dead fridges before coming to a shuddering, dusty halt.

'Oh dear,' said Griselda.

'Oh dear,' said Scarlet.

With a ghostly shimmer Gory swooped back down beside us, a triumphant smile on his face. 'Ye-eh! I done it!' he yelled. 'I stopped the lorry!'

'Yes, very nice,' said Scarlet. 'Unfortunately it was the *wrong* lorry!'

We pointed to where Baldy was busily reversing his lorry with Grandad on the back towards a huge pit in the ground, where an enormous crushing machine clattered away.

Little Alfie burst into tears. 'Mummy! Mummy!' he started wailing.

'Oh, Alfie, do shut up,' snapped Griselda, still cross with Gory for getting the wrong lorry.

We watched in horror as the lorry edged closer to the pit.

By now Mort had joined us from his hearse.

'Oh dear,' he sighed. 'How sad. How very sad. What a waste of a perfectly good coffin.'

Suddenly, the lorry stopped. The driver's door flew open and Baldy clambered down. He ran like mad towards the old caravan that served as an office.

'Mummy!' he screamed, casting a terrified look towards the gates. 'Mummy!'

We looked up and saw a tall figure swathed in bandages, striding towards us from the entrance to the dump.

'Mummy!' Little Alfie wailed, pointing a stubby finger at the figure. 'Mummy!'

'Oh heck, now I'm in trouble,' groaned Griselda. 'It's Alfie's mummy. It's part of her powers. If he yells loudly enough, she can hear him up to a radius of about fifty kilometres. And then she spirits herself to him. Now she'll tell me off for not looking after him properly. It's all your fault, Jonathan.'

'Hey, are we going to rescue Mr Leech or what?' asked Crombie.

Leaving Little Alfie to his mummy's embrace, we ran across the tarmac to Baldy's lorry.

We clambered up into the skip, and between us, got the coffin down on to the ground. Gory found a bit of old metal and we prised off the lid. There, inside, snoring away peacefully with a smile on his face, was Grandad.

Chapter 21

GRANDAD TOOK SOME WAKING up, and even then he wasn't that keen on getting out of his coffin. So, as Little Alfie's mummy wanted a lift back down into Goolish and it was a bit full inside Mort's hearse, we put the coffin up on to the roof with Grandad still in it. Once Griselda had given him his false fangs back, he began to liven up.

While Mort was tying the knots, I looked round and saw Scarlet by my side. She shook her head and looked at me, sadly.

'What a terrible thing to do! Putting your own Grandfather on a skip.'

'If it wasn't for us, you'd be on a murder rap,' muttered Gory, who had sneaked up behind me.

'I didn't know he was in the coffin!' I protested. 'I thought if I got rid of his coffin and stuff he wouldn't be tempted into vampiring any more.'

'You can't stop him being a vampire! You shouldn't *want* to stop him being a vampire. Why can't you accept him for what he is?' said Scarlet. She sighed. 'Why can't you accept yourself for what you are?'

Mort blew the hooter on the hearse and beckoned to us. He was ready to go, which was lucky, really, as Baldy and his mate – who had crashed into the fridges – were making their way to us waving metal pipes and hammers.

'Thanks for saving Grandad,' I said to Scarlet.

'Come on,' she replied with a smile, 'let's get going before I have to start howling to try and frighten those two idiots off.'

We were driving back to Goolish and were just coming up to the woods on the hill when I saw a car coming towards us. It was a silver cabriolet: Tiffany and her mum. Scarlet saw them too.

'It's twitty Tiffany and her mum, guys!' said Scarlet. 'Let's all give them a big wave, shall we?'

They wound down the windows and waved like mad as the cabriolet sped past. When I peeped out of the back window, I saw the cabriolet weaving all over the road. No doubt Mrs Bliss had seen Grandad in his coffin on the roof and was reaching for her digital camera. I wondered if Tiffany had seen me. If she had, it would certainly make for an interesting conversation next time I saw her. I wasn't going to let that worry me now. Now I was happy: I had got Grandad back.

When we arrived back at Drac's Cottage we got Grandad down off the roof.

'Thanks for the lift, Mort,' said Scarlet.

Mort shrugged his heavy shoulders. 'When you told me one of my lovely coffins was on a *skip* . . . ! Well . . . what else could I do?'

Mort drove Little Alfie and his mummy home and Grandad took his coffin back into the cottage. I was left alone with the Fang Gang. I kicked a few stones around, keeping my eyes firmly on the ground.

'I guess I owe you all a big thank you,' I said. 'For helping me out like that.'

'I guess you do,' said Gory.

'It was Little Alfie and his mummy, who really saved your grandad,' said Crombie.

'Perhaps Little Alfie should be allowed to join the Fang Gang,' suggested Scarlet.

'No!' chorused Griselda, Crombie and Gory.

'Look,' I said. 'I know I've said some pretty stupid things, but this has all come as a bit of a shock to me. I was wondering . . . you know. . .'

'Wondering you know what?' asked Griselda, with a sly grin.

'Well . . . about . . .'

'What?!'

But I couldn't bring myself to ask, just in case they all said: 'No!'

There was a silence that seemed to go on for ever.

'Oh, for goodness' sake,' said Scarlet. 'All those in favour of Jonathan joining the Fang Gang?'

Scarlet, Griselda and Crombie the Zombie raised their hands.

'Gory, why must you always be such a miserable little twit?'

'Have you ever heard of a cheerful ghoul?' asked Gory, slowly raising his hand.

'Welcome to the Fang Gang, Jonathan,' said Scarlet.

It was the first time I'd shaken hands with a werewolf.

Chapter 22

'TWO SAUSAGES OR THREE?'
asked Grandad, as we sat down to
breakfast.

'Four, please,' I said.

'Vampire sausages, these.'

I gulped.

'Full of all the goodness a growing vampire
like yourself needs. Blood, gristle, brains . . .
Don't worry, boy, not *human* blood. I wouldn't

give you that. Not yet. Any more than I'd give a boy your age a bottle of beer or a gin and tonic.'

'Do you think those sausages helped me run so fast?'

'I'm sure they did.'

'Grandad, I'm really sorry I threw your coffin on to that skip.'

'Oh, don't worry about it, boy.'

'I didn't know you were in it. I was only trying to get rid of the coffin.'

'You thought you could get rid of what I am and who I am just like that?'

I nodded.

'Never mind. All's well that ends well, eh? At least we understand each other now, don't we?'

'I think so. What I don't understand is, if you're a vampire and I'm a vampire, how come Dad isn't a vampire?'

Grandad shrugged. 'The gifts sometimes skip a generation,' he said. 'Like Scarlet's mum. She's no more a werewolf than I am. And, of course, if one of your parents is from the dark side and the other is from the light side, that can affect things too.'

'No wonder Dad wasn't keen for me to stay with you.'

I tucked into my sausages and Grandad picked up the morning paper. I saw the headline on the front page:

DAILY WAIL
PENSIONER HOODIES HIT GOOLISH!
TV REPORTER IN OAP HORROR!

'Grandad,' I said, sternly. 'You're on the front page.'

Grandad looked at the front page. 'Me?'

'Yes, Grandad, you. When you scared that woman and her daughter by leering at them through their windscreen.'

'Eh?' said Grandad, dreamily. 'I'm sure I don't know what you're talking about.'

'Yes, you do, Grandad. I was there.'

Grandad gasped.

'See where it says: "*TV reporter Belinda Bliss*

was with her daughter and a friend"?' I went on. 'Well, *I* was that friend.'

'You, boy?'

'Yes. Except I'm *not* her friend.'

'It says you are, in the paper,' said Grandad.

'It doesn't matter what it says in the paper.'

'Quite right, boy. Let's ignore the whole story, shall we?'

'No, Grandad! It happened,' I said, with a sigh. 'Tell me, why do you have to go round scaring people?'

Grandad sighed. 'You're right. I shouldn't, I suppose. But it's . . . such *fun*! I mean, you should've seen that snooty woman's face!'

'I *did* see that snooty woman's face,' I replied. 'The thing is, being an investigative journalist she might decide to start investigating life on the dark side in Goolish. If she does, we'll all be in serious trouble. We've all got to be careful.'

'Difficult to be careful when you're my age,' replied Grandad. He smiled. 'Now, here's a joke. What do you call a dog with no legs?'

I shook my head.

'It doesn't matter what you call him, because he won't come, anyway!' chortled Grandad. 'Oh, that's a wicked one, that is. Another sausage, boy?'

I couldn't answer. I was laughing too much. He was so funny, so infuriating, so outrageous. In fact, he was a proper grandad.

After breakfast the postman called with a package for me. I took it upstairs to my room. Inside was a letter and a postcard. I read the letter first:

HM Prison Crookstown

Dear Jonathan

Well, here I am in prison. The judge was very nice. He let me off the charge of ramming Mrs Rhode-Hogg on account of the fact that she's a miserable old biddy and deserved all she got. He couldn't let me off the charge of grievous bodily harm to a frozen turkey though. So here I am. The Governor says I'll be out in a month with good behaviour, but I've never bothered about being good and I'm too old to start now, so I'll probably stay here for my whole sentence which is three months.

Your ever-loving gran

Then I read the postcard:

Dear Jonathan.
I hope you are well. Your dad and I aren't. In fact, we have been quite sick. This isn't anything to do with the rough weather at sea, but because one of the conditions of winning the prize from 'Muck-In-A-Minute Meals' is that we have to eat their gruesome instant dinners every evening. We haven't seen any penguins yet, but the Captain says that's because we're still only off the coast of France. Give my love to your gran and to Paul and Barry the garden gnomes.

Lots of love, Mum xx
PS Don't forget to wash your feet.

I went upstairs and wrote another list:

LIFE WITH GRANDAD LIST

Plusses	Minuses
Grandad	Tiffany Bliss
No yucky moments	
(e.g. Mum and Dad)	
Nice letters from Gran	
Sausages	
The Fang Gang (well, most of them)	

It was the coolest list ever. Provided Gran kept her word and didn't behave herself in prison, I had a whole three months staying with Grandad and hanging about with the Fang Gang.

It was a shame about the one awful item in the 'minuses' column. But the truth was that sometime, very soon, I, Jonathan Leech, Trainee Vampire and member of the Fang Gang, would have to face Tiffany Bliss, Wannabe Vampire Slayer.

Things could soon start getting very ugly indeed.